TWENTIETH CENTURY FOX PRESENTS

ICE AGE™

STOP AND SMELL THE DANDELION

A Scratch-and-Sniff Book

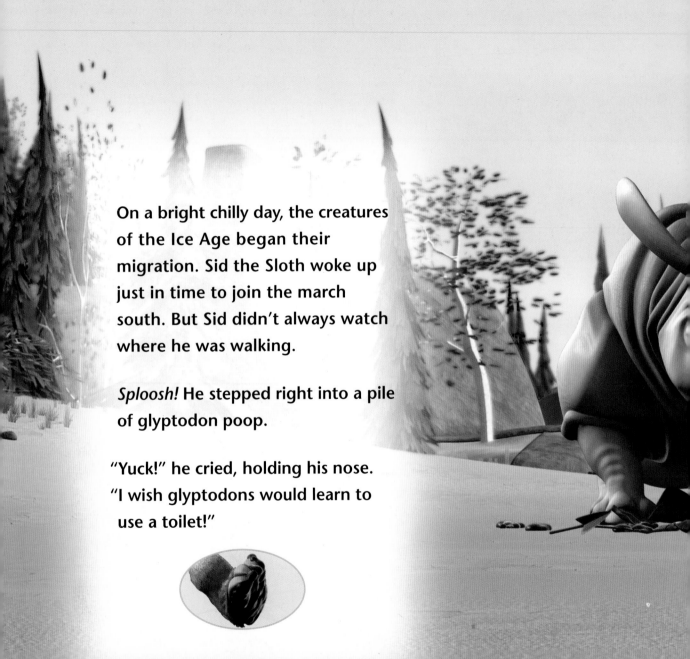

On a bright chilly day, the creatures of the Ice Age began their migration. Sid the Sloth woke up just in time to join the march south. But Sid didn't always watch where he was walking.

Sploosh! He stepped right into a pile of glyptodon poop.

"Yuck!" he cried, holding his nose. "I wish glyptodons would learn to use a toilet!"

While Sid was shaking the poop off his foot, he spotted a fragrant yellow dandelion. "Oh, yummo!" he shouted. "I thought these were all gone!"

He snatched up the flower and popped it into his mouth. What a perfect snack!

Between bites, Sid looked up and saw two rhinos named Carl and Frank. "Carl," Frank said, fuming, "he ruined our salad." Sid knew he was in trouble now.

He realized he had eaten their one and only flower. "My mistake. Let me make it up to you," he told them. Sid picked up a pinecone and sniffed. "Mmm. Smells delicious. Here. Have some!" he said as he stuffed a handful into Carl's mouth and ran away.

Carl and Frank charged after Sid. Luckily, Sid smacked right into the backside of Manfred, a gigantic woolly mammoth. Since Manny saved Sid's life, Sid decided to stick with him.

During their journey, Sid and Manny found a human baby named Roshan. "We've got to bring this baby back to his tribe," Sid cried.

But Manny didn't want a baby around. He thought Roshan would be too much trouble. Sure enough, Roshan flung a smelly, slimy fish right onto Manny's trunk!

Maybe if Diego, the saber-toothed tiger, joined the herd, things wouldn't get so out of hand.

But of course things got out of hand. Sid soon bumped into an old girlfriend named Sylvia. She was crazy about Sid and wanted him to head south with her. But Sid wasn't ready for such a big step. He was always trying to get away from her. If only he had hidden from her when he first got a whiff of her strong perfume. Her scent always filled the air.

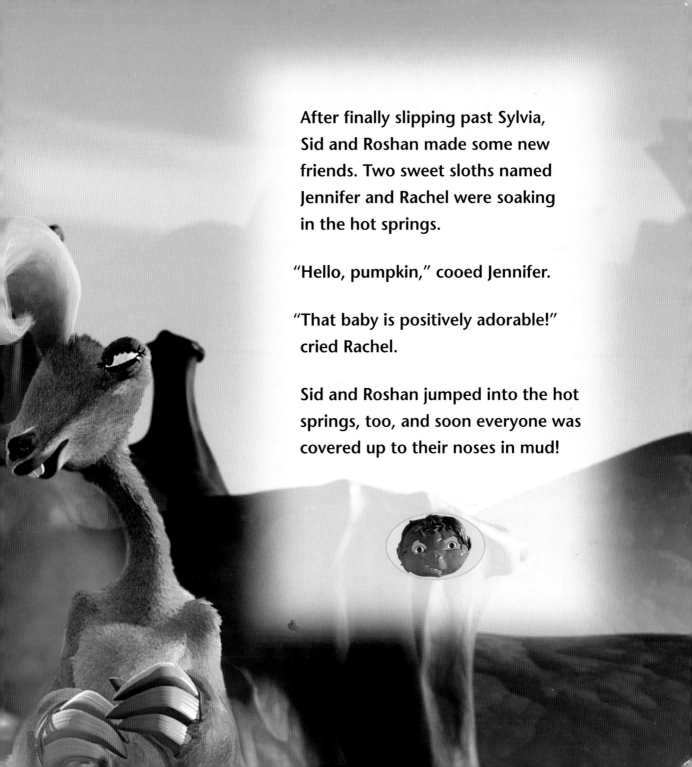

After finally slipping past Sylvia, Sid and Roshan made some new friends. Two sweet sloths named Jennifer and Rachel were soaking in the hot springs.

"Hello, pumpkin," cooed Jennifer.

"That baby is positively adorable!" cried Rachel.

Sid and Roshan jumped into the hot springs, too, and soon everyone was covered up to their noses in mud!

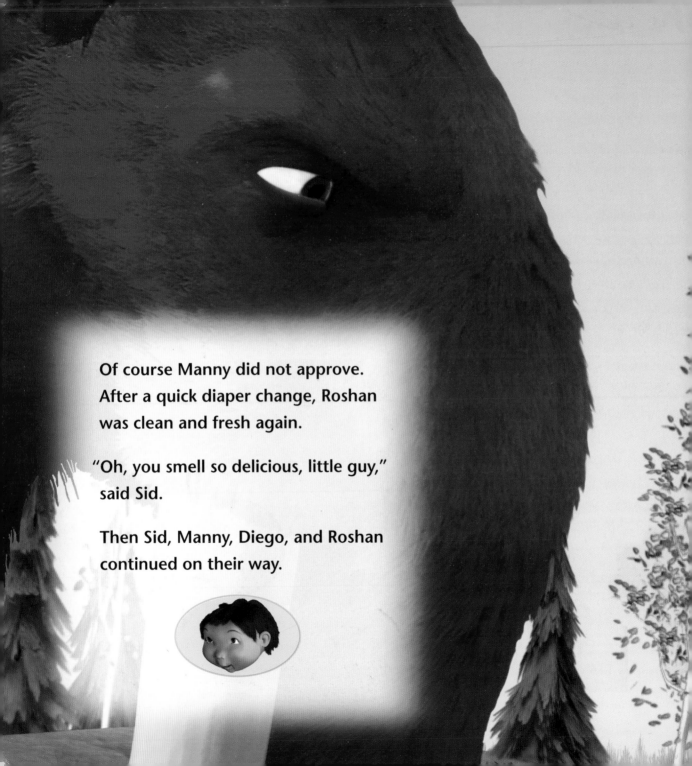

Of course Manny did not approve.
After a quick diaper change, Roshan
was clean and fresh again.

"Oh, you smell so delicious, little guy,"
said Sid.

Then Sid, Manny, Diego, and Roshan
continued on their way.

The smell of cedar filled the afternoon air. The trio's journey was almost over. Soon Roshan would be reunited with his father.

"Good-bye, little guy," Sid will say, his eyes misty with tears.

"I'll miss you, kid," Manny will add.

Even though Sid was sad that he and the others would have to part from Roshan when they reached the human camp, he knew they would all be friends forever.